The Sugar Snow Spring

The Sugar

Words and Pictures by
Lillian Hoban

Harper & Row, Publishers
New York
Evanston
San Francisco
London

Snow Spring

THE SUGAR SNOW SPRING
Copyright © 1973 by Lillian Hoban

LIBRARY OF CONGRESS CATALOG CARD NUMBER: 72-9866
TRADE STANDARD BOOK NUMBER: 06-022333-2
HARPERCREST STANDARD BOOK NUMBER: 06-022334-0

FIRST EDITION

For Esmé and her horse, Shandy,
in whose feed-bin we found Everett

The Sugar Snow Spring

A shrill wind whistled in the chimney of the hollow-stump house where Everett Mouse and his wife Henrietta lived with their son Oscar. It was an unusually cold winter, and Everett and Oscar worked hard every day to keep the icebox and the pantry shelves well-stocked. Henrietta made them backpacks out of scraps of old feed bags, but most days they came home with their packs half full and had to go out again in the evening. Supplies were short because of the heavy drifts of snow. Getting them was made more difficult by the new cat who had come to live in the barn.

Henrietta did as much as she could to help, knitting extra-warm mufflers and mittens, but she was very busy preparing for the arrival of a new baby. She made tiny little vests and bonnets and booties, some in pink, "In case it's a girl," she said, and some in blue, because it might be a boy. Everett promised to get some straw from the barn so that he could plait a little basket for the baby to sleep in.

"That darn cat doesn't let me get anywhere near the horse's bedding straw," he said. "But I'll get to it one of these days."

"It better be soon," said Henrietta. "Spring is almost here, and I just know this is a spring baby."

"Be a long time before spring," said Everett. "Sounds like it's blowing up another snowstorm right now."

The wind that was blowing down the chimney did have a smell of snow in it, and after supper Henrietta said anxiously, "I hope you don't have to go out again tonight. The cat always seems to catch more mice when it snows." It was true; that winter many mouse

homes were left fatherless after a snowstorm.

"We didn't bring in enough for tomorrow's
breakfast," said Everett. "Got to go out again
tonight."

"Do be careful," said Henrietta as she
helped them get their backpacks on.

Oscar and Everett made their usual rounds.
First, up to the house on the hill where they
frequently found bread crumbs scattered on
the snow for the chickadees.

"Fattest chickadees I've ever seen," grumbled Everett as he put some crumbs into
Oscar's pack. "They leave precious little for
us mice."

Then they went over to the barn behind
the house. Here they were in constant dan-
ger. It took expert teamwork to outwit Ethel
the cat and get into the grain bin.

Oscar went into the barn first. He jumped
up and down on a loose floorboard as hard as
he could to get Ethel's attention. She had
been dozing on a pile of feed bags, but she was

11

on the alert immediately, her back arched,
her tail high, and her whiskers quivering.
Oscar waited a moment to be sure she'd seen
him. Then he ran into the tack room with
Ethel hot on his trail.

Everett slipped into the barn. He made his
way quickly to the storeroom, ran up the side
of the feed bin, and jumped on all fours into
the grain where he at once set to work filling
his backpack.

Meanwhile Oscar raced around the tack
room creating an obstacle course for the cat.
He skittered under the rake, between the
tines of the pitchfork, and up and over the

saddle rack. Then, just as Ethel was about to pounce, he dodged through a knothole in the back wall.

Everett, having filled his pack, slid down the side of the bin and crept quietly over to the horse's stall. "If I could just get enough bedding straw to start making the basket," he said, "Henrietta would feel easier in her mind."

He pulled some of the cleaner straw out of the pile and began to look for the long supple pieces that he needed. Suddenly he saw the shadow of Ethel's head loom on the back wall of the stall. Everett dove under the bedding straw and held his breath. The cat walked past the stall and headed for the feed bags. She yawned, stretched lazily, curled up with her tail under her chin, and settled down for a nap.

Everett quietly slipped out of his hiding place and, keeping under cover in the dark shadows along the walls, ran out of the barn. Oscar was waiting for him behind the woodpile.

"We'll have to find a new way to fool Ethel," said Everett. "I need more time to get the bedding straw."

A mixture of rain and fat wet snowflakes was coming down as they started home.

"Ma was right about the weather," said Oscar, sloshing along. "I hope she's right about spring coming soon, too."

"Your mother is 'most always right," said Everett. "I'd better get to work on the basket for the baby or—"

"Help!" cried Oscar. He had slipped on the glazed surface of the snow and fallen into a deep bootprint in the path.

"Can you climb out?" asked Everett anxiously as he peered down at him.

"The sides are too steep and slippery," said Oscar.

"I'll try to reach you," said Everett, and he lay down on his stomach and stretched as far as he could into the hole. It was no use. The bootprint was much too deep.

"Now don't be scared," said Everett, "and don't make a sound or the cat will come after you. I'm going home to get some rope—be back in a jiffy."

Oscar settled down into the toe of the bootprint; it seemed less damp there. But in a very short time the rain and sleet made a large enough puddle so that his feet got quite damp and he started to shiver. Then he sneezed.

"*Gesundheit,*" said a voice.

"Wh-who's that?" asked Oscar.

"I'm your friendly Easter Bunny," said the voice, "out to take a census on how many Easter eggs I have to deliver this year."

"Easter eggs in the snow?" asked Oscar.

"It's sugar snow," said the rabbit. "Spring's just around the corner. What are you doing down there anyhow? You'll catch your death of a cold."

"I fell in," said Oscar, "and Dad's gone home to get a rope to haul me out."

"Then I better let you stay down there till he gets back," said the rabbit. "I hope he hurries. Spring's a bad time to be laid up with the croup. Well, got to be going now. Still have a lot more censusing to do." And he hopped off into the dark.

Oscar's teeth were chattering, and he tried to draw his feet up under him. "That Easter Bunny must be crazy," he thought. "What did he mean by sugar snow, anyway?" He caught a flake of snow on the tip of his tongue. "Doesn't taste sweet to me."

"Oscar," called Everett, "I've got the rope. You catch hold of the end of it and I'll haul you up." Everett anchored his feet firmly behind a rock, and pulled a wet, bedraggled Oscar out of the bootprint.

"What's sugar snow?" asked Oscar between sneezes as they walked home.

"That's when it snows after the sap starts running in the maple trees," said Everett. "It means spring is just around the corner."

"Then the Easter Bunny was right," said Oscar.

"What bunny?" asked Everett as they walked down the path to the house. An anxious Henrietta opened the door and immediately wrapped Oscar in a towel.

"I think the boy's caught a fever," said Everett. "He's talking nonsense about an Easter Bunny."

"Well, what do you expect?" scolded Henrietta. "I'm sure he's caught the croup. Hurry and put up the croup kettle."

Henrietta helped Oscar undress, and got him into bed with a hot-water bottle. Then she brought him a steaming cup of tea with lots of honey.

"Got to get the straw for the basket," said Oscar as he was drifting off to sleep. "Spring is almost here."

"He's such a good boy," said Henrietta, touching her apron to her eyes. "Here he is practically delirious, and he's thinking of a bed for the baby."

The next morning Oscar felt awful. His nose was running, he had a wheezy cough, and his head felt like a pumpkin.

"You'd better not make the rounds today," his father said kindly.

"But Dad, how will you get the bedding straw without me to decoy Ethel? The rabbit said it was almost spring—"

"Now you stop this nonsense about a rabbit," his father said sternly. "Any self-respecting rabbit would have been holed up last night."

"But this was the Easter Bunny," said Oscar, "and he said it was sugar snow and spring's just around the corner."

"That's enough now," said Everett. "It won't be spring for a good long while. Plenty of time to make a basket." He put on his backpack and went out.

"I hope the chickadees leave lots of bread crumbs," said Oscar later in the day. He was sitting up, snugly wrapped in his bathrobe, his feet in a tub of hot water. "I hope Dad doesn't have to go in the barn at all. Ethel is so fast, he really needs me to get her out of the way."

"Well now, don't you worry," said Henrietta, looking out of the window. "Your Dad's always been a good provider, and I expect he'll be able to do by himself until your cold's better." She was watching the sun set and worriedly thinking that Everett should be home by now.

Everett did not come home that night, or the next day, or the next night either. Ma tried her best to act cheerful, but she sighed frequently and often paused at the window and looked out. It was a small heavy-hearted Oscar who went to make the rounds alone the third day after Everett's disappearance. The sun was shining, the air was warm and balmy, and the snow was thawing fast. Oscar, looking at the trickling rivulets of melting ice, thought sadly, "Dad's gone, it's almost spring, and there's no basket for the baby."

He trudged up the hill, stopping to watch a robin pull a bit of yarn from a twig. The yarn was stuck fast, and the robin almost fell over backward when it suddenly came loose.

"Nesting time, you know," said the robin with an embarrassed twitch of her tail, and she flew off.

Oscar gathered the bread crumbs that the chickadees had left, each in its own little depression in the snow. They were sodden and heavy, and weighed down his backpack. Farther up the hill a squirrel was chattering angrily at a cardinal who was pecking at a bird feeder hung in the tree. The cardinal nervously scattered birdseed and grain out of the feeder, and Oscar gathered it all up.

His pack was full now, and he could have gone home. With only two mouths to feed, it was easy to keep the pantry well-stocked. But Oscar decided to go up to the barn and try his luck at getting some straw. He slipped through the barn door, and keeping in the shadows, edged toward the horse's stall.

Suddenly he froze. There in the door of the storeroom was Ethel. She was crouched down ready to spring, her attention riveted to the grain bin. Oscar could hear a faint whispery sound coming from the bin. Just then a loose floorboard creaked under Oscar's feet, and Ethel turned, saw him, and like a flash came after him.

Oscar ran out of the barn as fast as he could, his backpack slapping heavily against him with each step. He flung himself down the hill, slipping and skidding in the slush. The cat was gaining on him and he was out of breath. Oscar was sure that she would get him. "What will Ma do without me or Dad," he thought, "and no one to make a basket for the baby?" He exerted every ounce of strength, but he was no match for the cat.

Just as he felt Ethel's hot breath on his tail, he was suddenly jerked off his feet and pulled into a briar bush.

"Well if it isn't the young mouse who was sneezing in the snow!" said the rabbit. For it was he who had pulled Oscar into the bush. "You *are* one for getting into trouble, aren't you. Your cold all gone now?" he asked kindly.

Oscar could scarcely talk, he was breathing so hard and his heart was pounding so fast. "Thank you, yes," he said as soon as he had caught his breath. "*It's* better, but everything else is worse."

"Things aren't that bad," said the rabbit. "The cat won't hang around here for long. She knows better than to get tangled up in a briar bush."

"It's not just the cat," said Oscar, and he was so tired and worried that he began to cry.

"There now," said the rabbit, giving Oscar a large handkerchief. "Suppose you tell me all about it."

Between sobs and sniffles, and with frequent pauses to blow his nose, Oscar told the rabbit all about Dad's disappearance, and Ma's new baby almost here, and no basket for it to sleep in, and no way of getting the straw to make the basket now that Dad was gone.

The rabbit looked more and more thoughtful as Oscar talked, and occasionally said, "Hmm," or, "Well, well." When Oscar finished, the rabbit patted him kindly on the shoulder, and said, "It'll be all right, you wait and see. Your ma's going to have a bed for that baby to sleep in, I know it. And here's something to cheer you up right now." He reached into his back pocket and got out a jelly bean and gave it to Oscar.

"Cat's gone," he said brightly, looking out of the briar bush. "You can run along home now and take care of your ma. You tell her not to worry now; it's not good for her to be upset in her condition." He patted Oscar on the head, gave him another jelly bean, and shoved him gently out of the briar bush.

When Oscar got home he helped his mother unload the backpack and get supper ready. He didn't tell her what the rabbit had said, because then he would have to tell her about almost getting caught by the cat. "And the rabbit said not to worry her in her condition," he thought. So he kept it to himself, and hoped the rabbit was right about the bed for the baby.

Oscar was very tired that evening and went to bed early. It seemed to him that he had just fallen asleep, when he heard Ma say, "Oscar, I think you better go get Dr. Pfeffer-Mouse, and before you go, put up a kettle of water to boil."

He pulled his clothes on, put the kettle up to boil, and ran through the moonlit night all the way to the doctor's house.

"Babies always being born in the middle

of the night," grumbled Dr. Pfeffer-Mouse
sleepily to Oscar as Mrs. Pfeffer-Mouse
helped him on with his coat.

"I hope you get back in time to go to church
in the morning," said Mrs. Pfeffer-Mouse.
"It's Easter Sunday."

"That's right," said Dr. Pfeffer-Mouse as
he collected his little black bag and his hat.
"Nothing but snow and ice till yesterday,
and here we are right smack into Easter."

Oscar wished Dr. Pfeffer-Mouse would

walk a little faster. But the Doctor just ambled along as though Ma weren't at home right now, about to have a baby. "Yes," the Doctor was saying, "I always like to go around to the Sunday School room on Easter Sunday. There's generally quite a few jelly beans left behind. I'm very fond of jelly beans."

Oscar had forgotten that there still was no basket for the baby. But when he heard the words "jelly beans" he remembered the rabbit, and how he'd said not to worry.

"That rabbit may have been right about the sugar snow," Oscar thought sadly, "but he's all wrong about the basket. I wish Dad were here. *He'd* know what to do."

The sky was rosy with dawn as Oscar and the doctor came down the path to the hollow-stump house. Once Dr. Pfeffer-Mouse got inside, he briskly ordered Oscar to get towels and soap and a basin of hot water. Then he disappeared into Ma's room.

Oscar hurried around getting everything ready. He was reaching into the cupboard for the towels when he heard a strange wheezing thumping sound at the front door. He was about to investigate when the door flew open and an object came hurtling across the floor. "Oh!" cried Oscar in delight. "Oh my! Oh my!"

For there in the center of the floor, practically at his feet, was the dearest smallest basket he had ever seen. It was filled with soft, pale-green wisps of shiny rabbit grass, and bedded down in it were jelly beans and a tiny chocolate Easter egg.

"Aren't you going to help me into the house?" said a familiar voice. Wedged into the open doorway was a very stout mouse. "Don't stand there with your mouth hanging open, boy," he said. "I'm stuck. Come pull me in."

"It's Dad!" gasped Oscar.

With much pulling and yanking on Oscar's part, and a great deal of wheezing and groaning on Dad's, he finally came unplugged like a cork from a bottle. Oscar helped Dad to his chair, and eased him out of his coat, which seemed to have grown several sizes too small.

"I never thought I'd make it," said Dad, heaving a sigh of relief. He eased himself into a more comfortable position. "For three days and three nights I've done nothing but eat." And he told Oscar that the cat had spotted him as he was about to go into the storeroom. He'd run up the side of the grain bin as fast as

he could and jumped in. He had plummeted
to the bottom of the bin like a stone, the
grain closing in over him.

"I had to *eat* my way clear of that grain,"

he groaned. "It's a lucky thing that the cat wasn't around when I finally got out. I was so stuffed it took me half the night to get down the hill. Just as I was coming up to the briar bush Ethel saw me, and if it hadn't been for your friend the Easter Bunny, I'd be a dead mouse. He was sitting in the briar bush getting ready to deliver Easter baskets, and he yanked me in.

"'You're the second mouse this week I've saved from that cat,' the rabbit told me. 'The first one was wearing a backpack too, but he was just a little fellow. You two aren't related, are you? He's a brave little fellow, so worried about his ma and not having a bed ready for the new baby.'

"'That's my son Oscar!' I said.

"'Well then, you can save me a trip,' the Easter Bunny told me. 'I've made up this basket special for him. I think he'll find it just the right size for the new baby—after he's through eating the jelly beans, of course!' And he gave me the basket to bring home for you. 'That's a fine boy you've got there,' he shouted after me. 'Keep more like him coming!'"

Just as Dad finished talking they heard a slapping sound from Ma's room and a shrill *eep—squeek*! Dr. Pfeffer-Mouse came out of Ma's room beaming. "Well, young man," he said, "you've got a new baby brother." His eyes fell on the tiny Easter basket. "What do you know, my favorite flavors of jelly beans. Couldn't ask for better pay." He popped them

into his mouth. "Wouldn't be good for you anyhow, Everett," he said. "You'd better be watching your weight. Seem to have gotten quite stout since the last time I saw you." And he put on his coat and hat, got his little black bag, and left.

Everett and Oscar tiptoed into Ma's room carrying the basket between them. There in Ma's arms was the tiniest baby mouse, wearing a little blue vest and booties. Ma's eyes were closed and she looked all happy and peaceful. "I've got a surprise for you," said Oscar. And when Ma's eyes flew open she saw Dad and the basket at the same time.

"Oh," whispered Ma, "now everything is perfect!"

There was much rejoicing in the hollow-stump house that day. For supper, Oscar and Ma shared the chocolate Easter egg; Dad said he really didn't care for any, thanks just the same.

That night, Oscar's new baby brother was carefully tucked into his own tiny basket, and there he slept very contentedly.

About the Author-Artist

Lillian Hoban has illustrated many distinguished picture books, including the popular "Frances" stories by Russell Hoban. She is the author-illustrator of *Arthur's Christmas Cookies,* an *I Can Read* Book which is a favorite of beginning readers.

There are four Hoban children—Phoebe, Brom, Esmé, and Julia. Esmé had a horse who in turn had a feed bin, where, one day, Lillian discovered Everett Mouse—and the idea of the story of *The Sugar Snow Spring.*

E
Hob

Hoban, Lillian
The sugar snow spring

9/10